ORCA
YOUNG
READERS

Addison Addley

AND THE TRICK OF THE EYE

MELODY DEFIELDS McMILLAN

ORCA BOOK PUBLISHERS

Library and Archives Canada Cataloguing in Publication

McMillan, Melody DeFields, 1956-

Addison Addley and the trick of the eye / Melody DeFields McMillan.

ISBN 978-1-55469-189-0

I. Title.

PS8625.M54A66 2009   jC813'.6   C2009-903347-X

First published in the United States, 2009
Library of Congress Control Number: 2009929318

Summary: Addison's mother wants to move, so Addison uses optical illusions and his own overheated imagination to convince her to stay in their old house.

Orca Book Publishers gratefully acknowledges the support for its publishing programs provided by the following agencies: the Government of Canada through the Book Publishing Industry Development Program and the Canada Council for the Arts, and the Province of British Columbia through the BC Arts Council and the Book Publishing Tax Credit.

Typesetting by Bruce Collins
Cover artwork by Peter Ferguson
Author photo by Justin McMillan

ORCA BOOK PUBLISHERS
PO Box 5626, STN. B
VICTORIA, BC CANADA
V8R 6S4

ORCA BOOK PUBLISHERS
PO Box 468
CUSTER, WA USA
98240-0468

www.orcabook.com
Printed and bound in Canada.
Printed on 100% PCW recycled paper.

12 11 10 09 • 4 3 2 1

To my little family and my big family

Chapter One

Sometimes, you've just got to expect the unexpected. That's what I should have been doing last Sunday when Mom dropped the bombshell on me. It wasn't a big bombshell, just four little words. Four little words too many.

"We need to move," she said.

I choked. My raspberry smoothie didn't taste so smooth anymore.

I was right in the middle of adding peanut-butter chips to the grocery list. First I thought maybe she was just trying to scare me into doing a better job of being in charge of the weekly budget. Ever since I had a math catastrophe at school, she's been making me keep the budget. She tells me how much we spend, and I record it. I'm in charge of figuring out what percentage we spend on each category, like food or entertainment. Mom likes to analyze things. You'd think she would have analyzed me enough by now to know that I'm not great at numbers. Besides, if it were up to me, I'd spend a bigger percentage on entertainment. I'd buy some new video games and invite my friends over. They'd bring a bunch of chips and pop, so that would take care of the food percentage too. Mom doesn't usually try to scare me though, because she knows I'm not much afraid of anything. I'm probably the bravest guy in my grade-five class.

Maybe I'd heard her wrong.

"Move, like in moving the furniture again?" I asked hopefully. Last summer we had moved the old couch fourteen times to get it to look just right in the newly painted living room. That old couch had ended up exactly where it started, right up against the window. My back ached just thinking about moving it again, but if it was a choice of moving the couch or moving me, the couch was the hands-down winner.

Mom shook her head as she dished up a bowl of vegetarian chili.

Maybe Mom's astronomy club was doing weird things to her brain again. Sometimes she thinks too much. She was probably worried that the stars weren't lined up right and that we needed to be in a different place in case a meteoroid came crashing down. She's always second-guessing herself. Or third- or fourth-guessing. She really thought too hard the time we painted the living room. I thought her head was going to explode. She covered the entire wall in little paint-sample chips and left it that way for six months. She couldn't decide on a color. Even after we painted it, she couldn't decide on the color and thought we should repaint it. Then she thought people would think we were crazy to paint the same wall twice in two days. We never did repaint it, but I still catch her staring at it sometimes. Personally I would have just left all of those little paint chips up there. They would have saved me a lot of work.

The astronomy angle gave me an idea. "You mean move, like how the earth moves around the sun? We're moving all the time, right?" I'd picked up a couple of things from all her star talk, which surprised me because usually things like that just float right out of my brain. I have a problem remembering school stuff too.

Unless it's important, like how many times I can hand in my homework late before I get a detention. Mom shook her head again.

I tried one last time. "You mean move, like we're moving up in the world, getting rich and famous?" That would be great. Of course I already knew that I would be rich and famous one day for my incredible inventions, but it would be nice to see Mom get rich too. Maybe if she studied the night sky long enough, she might just discover a new planet. Then she'd have to go on TV and talk about it and maybe someone would pay her a lot of money to write a book.

This time Mom groaned.

"That's just it," she explained. "We're not getting rich and famous. Not that I'd really want to be famous. But having a bit more money would be nice."

She swept her hand in front of her. "This house," she said emphatically, "is just too big. Too big for the two of us. There's just too much to take care of."

Too big? Was I hearing things? A kingdom is too big. A castle is too big. Even a dungeon is too big. I looked around the kitchen. This house was definitely not too big. You could barely open the fridge door without hitting the kitchen table, where we ate all our meals. I guess we could be using the dining-room table, but it was the perfect place to store my comic books and Mom's star maps. The living room was just the right width for me to do ten kicking karate chops when I was playing my *Ancient Warrior* video game. I didn't understand how she could think the house was too big. Maybe she meant there were too many rooms. The only time we used the guest bedroom downstairs was when we had guest mice. We needed that room. Where else were the mice supposed to stay when they got tired of sleeping in the attic?

The only thing that was really big was the yard. It was huge. I liked it that way, even though I complained about it when I had to cut the grass.

I took some pepperoni pieces that were hiding in my pocket and slipped them into my chili. Mom's vegetarian recipes sometimes needed an extra boost.

"For the same amount that we pay every month for this house, we could get a brand new place," she said as she sat down. "A smaller one, but one with less upkeep."

Upkeep? What was there to keep up? I was in charge of the lawn and the garbage. What else was there?

Mom could read my mind. "This house needs a complete makeover," she said. "I've been doing some things, but there's just too much work. Since your father left, I just can't keep up with everything."

Dad left us four years ago to start a new job in Australia. He'd traded us for a bunch of sheep, just like we were hockey cards. He must be super busy, because I hardly ever hear from him anymore. Dad never was great at fixing things anyway, so I didn't notice much difference in how the place looked now. I guess Mom looked more closely.

"The front door needs painting," she continued. "The shed siding is falling off. The deck needs staining. The lawn is filled with weeds. The window in the bedroom is cracked. The upstairs bathroom tap is leaking. The attic needs new insulation. The trees need cutting back. The porch stairs are sagging. The—"

"Okay, okay, I get the point," I interrupted. I still didn't get it really. All the things on her list added personality to the old place. "So you want a smaller place that has nothing broken." And no personality, I added silently.

"Well, speaking of smaller, there's a new development that's opening up next month across town," she said.

I didn't like the sound of the word *development*. It sounded too serious. What exactly was a *development* anyway?

"It's a new row of townhouses," Mom said, knocking over her cup of blueberry tea as she reached for a pen. She wiped up the mess with a paper towel and then started drawing on a clean one. She drew some rectangles and a squiggly line that was supposed to be a road. She pointed to the rectangles. "They're just the size we need, and the monthly payments would be slightly less than what I'm paying now. There's going to be an open house there in a few weeks. If everything looks good, I'd like to be first on the waiting list. Those units will go fast."

Townhouse? Was that like an apartment? Apartments were small. Very small. I couldn't imagine moving to something smaller than our house. My friend Sam's grandmother had an apartment. I couldn't think of anything smaller than that. Well, maybe a shoe box.

"It's close to the new industrial park," Mom continued.

Industrial park? Those two words didn't go together. "You mean where the new shoe factory is?"

I asked. There was no way on earth I was going to live near a shoe factory. I mean, how much soul could a shoe factory have? I liked that line. I'd have to use it on Mom if I couldn't get her to come to her senses.

How could she even think of leaving this place? There were so many memories. There were so many hiding places. There were so many holes in the lawn where I'd buried treasures like my first baby tooth and my 1920 penny. And what about my favorite pine tree? I'd almost burned it down when I was doing an experiment a couple of years ago. I'd accidentally set it on fire when I was trying to see if sparks fly like fireflies do. Turns out they don't. At least not ones made from burning popsicle sticks.

Mom put down her spoon and looked me straight in the eye. "I didn't want to alarm you, honey," she whispered, "but there's another reason for moving."

She glanced over her shoulder like someone was hiding behind the fridge.

"There's an intruder in our neighborhood. There have been two break-ins in the last two weeks. I just don't feel safe here anymore."

I felt a shiver go up my spine. I'd heard just about enough. I'm not good at math, but two houses in two weeks adds up to a lot of creepiness. Next week would be the third week. I'd have to make sure there wouldn't be a third break-in.

It was bad enough thinking about moving to a shoe box near a shoe factory, but now I also had to worry about some stranger prowling around our street. I'd have to move fast. It was time to make a plan, time to turn things around. And I knew just who to turn to.

Chapter Two

"Moving!" Sam cried as he dropped his fishing pole and box of worms. He shook his head like he didn't believe me. His glasses slid off his nose.

"Moving?" he yelled as he grabbed for them before they tumbled into the creek. "You're moving?" he asked as he fumbled around on the ground.

My friend Sam repeats things three times when he gets excited or nervous. I guess he was a little of both right now.

I reached down and grabbed his glasses. "Here you go," I said, picking off the two worms that were stuck to the lenses. I grabbed the other worms and stuck them back in Sam's box. I wouldn't need them today because I was going to try out my new lure instead.

"We've got to come up with a plan to change your mom's mind," Sam said. "You just can't move." He was pacing back and forth so fast I was sure he was going to fall into the creek. "Especially not to the new development. You'd be at a different school!"

I hadn't thought about that. I didn't want to think about that. I'd be like a fish out of water at that dumb school. Even their baseball team was dumb. The Westside Wildcats, or Whinycats, as we liked to call them, had a kitten as their mascot. I mean, really, who would have a kitten as a mascot unless you were a veterinarian or a pet-shop owner?

I cast my line out into the water and leaned back against the old oak tree. The creek was so shallow and the water was so clear you could easily see the bottom. I tried to imagine living in the new townhouse, walking to the new school. Then I tried not to imagine it. I decided to think about fish instead. That was easier. I put down my pole and closed my eyes.

Thinking about fish was a whole lot nicer than thinking about a shoe box.

It's a good thing Sam and I were able to think about fish, because that's about all we ever did with them. We sure couldn't catch them. I had a sneaking suspicion that nobody had ever caught a fish in that creek. It was fun trying though. Not to mention that the creek made a great hiding place from chores and annoying people.

Sam must have been thinking about annoying people too. "At least you'd be away from Tiffany," he said as he sat down on the bank. "But then you'd be at the same school as Tiffany's cousin."

If there was anyone more annoying than Tiffany Wilson, the meanest kid in my grade-five class, it was her cousin, Trent. He had just moved here last month. He thought he was the smartest kid on the planet, and the best baseball player this side of Mars, according to Tiffany. Whenever Tiffany took a break from bragging about herself, which wasn't very often, she bragged about Trent. I couldn't decide which was worse.

I didn't have much time to think about Trent, because suddenly I had a bite. At least I thought I had one. I'd left the pole lying on the ground, so I really couldn't tell if there had been a tug on it or not. But when I opened my eyes, the lure was sparkling at least a foot from where I had thrown it. Logically, something must have dragged it there.

A fish was probably waiting behind the big rock next to it, ready to pounce on it again. I'd have to move fast to catch it by surprise when it went for the lure again. My brain may not work too fast but it sure could outwit a fish. I knew that fish would be back. He wasn't there yet, but I bet he would be there in seconds. I'd use my incredible timing to pull it in just as it was going for the prize. Sometimes you've just got to take the gamble and trust yourself. I counted to three to give the fish time to come back. Then I stood up and yanked as hard as I could on the line. It came out easily. Too easily. It flew back and the hook just missed the tree—and Sam's nose.

Sam jumped up. "What are you doing?" he cried. "You could have sliced me open! You could have broken my glasses! You could have ripped out my hair!"

He stomped three times. "You didn't even have a bite," he said.

So much for logic. "The lure moved closer to that bank," I explained as I cast my line back into the shallow water. "I thought maybe a fish had pulled it there and was hiding behind that big rock. I was sure he would come back for it. He must have seen a better lure down the creek. Next time I'm using my worms."

You really couldn't go wrong with worms. They were the best. I don't know why I hadn't used them in the first place. The news about moving must have scrambled my brain and jumbled up my heart, because I was usually a pretty loyal worm-user. I hoped worms didn't have feelings. I didn't want them to feel left out.

Sam scratched his head while he peered into the creek. He bent down and looked some more. He thought for a minute, and then he nodded his head.

"Refraction," he said.

"Re—what?" I asked.

"Refraction. It's a science term. It's sort of like an optical illusion," he explained.

"You mean like a magician sort of thing?" I asked. I liked magicians. They tricked people and made it look easy. You could probably get pretty rich being a magician and not even have to do a lot of work. That sounded like my sort of job.

"Sort of," Sam said. "I guess you could say that. Refraction's cool. I read all about it in my dad's science magazine."

Why anyone would want to read a science magazine was beyond me. It was hard enough keeping up with my comic books.

"That lure is not where you think it is," Sam said, jumping up quickly. He pointed to the water. "You see, when light goes through the air, it goes in a straight line. When it passes from the air to the water though, it gets bent, or refracted."

Now it was my turn to scratch my head. Maybe Sam's brain was refracted. "How can light bend?" I asked. This just didn't make sense. That's the problem with having a best friend who's so smart. A lot of the time he just doesn't make sense. I don't hold that against him though. He comes in handy a lot.

"The air has a different density than the water," Sam said, practically bubbling over with enthusiasm. He likes having me around to explain things to. That's okay. I like to do my bit for our friendship. "When the light hits the water, it changes speed and bends."

He pointed to the lure glistening in the creek. "That lure is actually in a different spot than you think. The light makes it look like it's moved. If you looked at it from a different angle, like lower down, it would look like it moved again."

I still didn't get it. Did a fish look like it was in a different place than where it was too? How would an eagle catch a fish if it wasn't where it was supposed to be? Eagles didn't learn about laws of refraction.

Maybe this refraction stuff would explain why we'd never caught any fish. There had to be some sort of explanation, because I knew we were the best fishermen around. At least we were the best at trying to be. And we didn't have a lot of competition.

Sam swept his arm out in front of him as he got ready for his grand finale speech. "Things can appear totally different, depending on what angle you're looking at them from. I guess you really could call that an optical illusion."

I nodded, pretending I understood. By that time, though, I didn't care if I understood the facts. The only things I needed to know were jumping around in my brain like fish in a net.

Different angle + optical illusion = different look…

I suddenly saw my moving problem in a whole new light. I would create some optical illusions of my own. I'd fool Mom into thinking that our dumpy old house was actually a mansion, heck, a castle.

A small castle, mind you, since she didn't want anything too big.

That new development was going to look like a rundown little doghouse when I got finished painting it in a new light.

The only thing I hadn't figured out yet was what to do about the break-ins. I didn't think that I could make an optical illusion out of them. No matter what angle you looked at them from, break-ins were still scary.

Chapter Three

Paint, nails, Sam's old gaming system. We wrote a list on the way home after school the next day. Well, actually, Sam wrote while I listed. I didn't want to waste energy doing both things at once.

"Wait a second," Sam cried. "My old gaming system? How is that going to make your house look better?"

"Come on, Sam, think!" I urged. Sometimes Sam doesn't get my ideas too quickly. I thought great minds were supposed to think alike. Maybe Sam's wasn't so great after all.

"It's the illusion thing. The more stuff we cram into the house, the smaller it's going to seem, and the more Mom will realize that we really do need all that space," I explained. That and the fact that I'd been dying to try out Sam's system on my own, without him watching me. I needed to practice without pressure. Besides, he had a new system now anyway. He usually likes to keep his games and systems all lined up and locked away in the closet, in alphabetical order. I was sure he could let one go just this once. After all, it was an emergency.

"It'll just be for a couple of weeks," I promised. "I'll take really good care of it." I would. Taking really good care of video games was one thing I was great at.

"Keep writing," I said. "Garbage bags, shovel, hole digger."

"Hole digger? Isn't that the same as a shovel?" Sam asked.

"No, not at all. I've got big plans for the backyard. I'm going to turn it into a worm store. I don't want to dig up the whole yard with a big shovel. Little holes will do. The worms aren't that big. I think I can make a hole digger with a spike and some duct tape. I'll need something to tie it on to though. I'm sure Mom doesn't need her old canoe paddle anymore."

Sam nodded. "That's not a bad idea. You could make some extra money that way! You can also get rid of some weeds at the same time."

Now Sam was catching on. I liked the words *at the same time*. There was no use wasting energy when I could get two things done at once. The way I looked at it, I had three problems to solve. One, I had to get Mom to look at the house from a different angle; two, I had to make the street safer by solving the break-in mystery; and three, I had to come up with some money to give to Mom for the monthly budget. Mom and I had already talked about ways of making more money. I had one paper route. I didn't want to take on another one. Sometimes I was chased by a little dog with three legs and sometimes I was chased by a little kid throwing stones at my bike. Selling worms would be a dream job compared to that.

"Now, you start thinking of some ideas to spruce up the old house," I encouraged Sam. He was probably better at home improvement than me. He liked everything to be neat and clean. He wouldn't even get his fingernails dirty when we tried to see if mud stuck to rocks better than it did to our feet. I was better at the money-making ideas.

"Maybe we could phone one of those home-makeover shows on TV, and they could renovate the house for free," Sam suggested.

I shook my head. "No, Sam," I explained patiently. "Think about it. The whole house would look brand new when it was done. Then people would think we were rich. Then our house would be the next one broken into."

When we got to my house, we looked at it from across the street. Did you ever notice how things look better when you know you might not see them anymore? The house did look sort of old and lopsided, but I liked it that way. It was comfortable. The only thing that looked fresh were all the trees in the backyard. Trees always look good because they grow new leaves every spring. They've got it easy.

"We have to fool Mom into looking at the house from a different angle," I said. "We need something out front to catch her eye." I'd seen the pamphlet for the new development. It had a white picket fence, a statue of a fat lady in a toga and a big rose garden in front of it. I'd think of something better. I only had three weeks until the open house. I'd have to move fast.

"Yeah, you're right," Sam said. "If you had something out front to focus on, your house might just fade into the background. It's got something to do with perspective. I learned that at summer camp last year when we tried to draw a picture of the lake. We had to make the trees in the front of the picture bigger than the ones in the back so the ones in the back looked farther away. It's easy to trick your eye into believing things. Remember how we made those flip books when we were in grade three? We drew stick people on the corners of a pad of paper and then flipped through the sheets as fast as we could. It looked like the stick people were moving. We tricked our eyes into thinking they were."

Sam was squinting at the house. I guess that makes him think better. He was just about to say something when Tiffany popped into view. She'd just rounded the corner of our street. What a way to wreck the scenery. Her cousin, Trent, was with her. The only good thing I could say about Trent was that his hair wasn't as puffy as Tiffany's. Her head looks like a lampshade, and sometimes her face gets as red and shiny as a Christmas-tree bulb. That's why I called her The Lamp. Tiffany always tries to annoy me. She really doesn't have to try too hard though, because annoying me is the one thing that she's good at. She's mean to every single person she knows. Heck, she probably even taught that little kid how to throw stones at my bike.

"I don't blame them for staring," Tiffany said loudly to Trent. "If I lived in a house like that, I wouldn't be able to believe my own eyes either. What a dump!"

"Get lost, Tiffany," I said. "My house is better than yours, and you know it."

"Better in what way?" she asked. "Better because there's more room for the rats to run around in your backyard?"

"At least I have a backyard," I answered. "Yours is the size of a stamp. Which is about the size of your brain, so at least you match."

The Lamp snarled. "Yeah, well I'm glad I don't live on this creepy street. Becky's house has been broken into twice already."

So it was Becky's house. Both times. I guess they hadn't got what they wanted the first time. Poor Becky. She was so shy already. Now she was probably afraid of her own shadow. Becky is smart. She doesn't talk a lot about herself though. She doesn't need to. She's nice. Do you ever notice how nice people don't talk a lot about themselves? I talk a lot about myself, but usually it's just to Sam. I don't know if that makes me nice or not. There's no question when it comes to Tiffany though. She's definitely not.

It bugged me that The Lamp always seemed to know things before I did. Then again, her mother knew every bit of gossip in town, mostly because she started every rumor in town too.

"It wasn't really her house," Tiffany continued. "The first time it was her shed. Stuff had been moved around like somebody was looking for something. The next time, someone messed with the lock on the garage. They didn't get inside though. Becky's mother found a note near the trash can by the garage that said *eight cents*."

The garage. I'd never liked that creepy garage of Becky's. It was full of junk her family got at yard sales. Once I walked by when it was just getting dark and I thought I saw a moose hanging upside down in the garage. Turns out it was just an overstuffed chair with four pointed legs that had fallen sideways on the twisted wire frame of a lampshade. It must have been a Tiffany lampshade because it was really big. Those wires looked just like antlers, at least the antlers I've seen on cartoons. I've never seen a real moose.

I'd probably have to go to the zoo. Do they have moose at zoos?

Tiffany flipped her hair away from her face. I guess it was so we could see her rolling her eyes better. "Some people just don't have any common sense," she sneered. "Becky's family should have locked their shed. At least they locked their garage. I guess they've learned their lesson."

It was too bad Tiffany hadn't learned to put a lock on her mouth.

Trent spoke up. "*Eight cents*. It was probably just some little kid counting up his pennies to buy a pack of gum. You guys get scared over nothing."

I wondered if I could pay Tiffany and Trent eight cents to get lost. I doubted it. They probably couldn't count that high.

"Well, my street beats your street by a mile," I said. Sam nodded. Tiffany lived in a new house a few streets over, not far from the school. Every house on her street looked exactly the same, like a row of Monopoly houses all lined up neatly on one side of the board. The streets were all named after trees. Tiffany lived on Willow Street. Her hair looked like a bunch of willow branches after a tornado.

"Don't listen to them," Trent said to Tiffany. "They're just worried about the game next week."

Our team was playing the Whinycats on Saturday. Trent was the pitcher. Why he would think we'd be nervous was a mystery to me. We would beat them hands down. We always did. The Whinycats had only won two games in the last two years. I guess Trent thought he was going to be the new hero and turn the team around.

Just then Trent waved his hands around like some crazy magician and then tapped his thumb three times with his other thumb.

Tiffany laughed, and they walked away from us.

"Secret signals," Sam said. "He's probably going to use them at the game."

"Well, they can keep their dumb secret signals," I said. "We need to come up with some optical illusions. Some good ones." I watched Tiffany and Trent cross the street. They were still laughing. It was too bad that I couldn't think of an optical illusion to just make them disappear.

Chapter Four

"We need to come up with some money," our teacher said on Thursday morning.

No kidding, I thought. It's funny how Miss Steane can read my mind. I was just thinking the same thing. I needed to come up with some money so I could buy some paint for the front door and some wood for the steps. Personally I don't mind that you have to jump over two holes in the second step to get to the third step, but I guess Mom does.

The money wasn't pouring in yet from the worm farm. I'd dug fifty-seven holes in the backyard with my special canoe-paddle hole digger but so far I'd only found three worms. I'm not good at math, but even I knew that three worms wasn't a whole lot for fifty-seven holes. I'd have to find out what worms ate. Maybe I could lure them out with some good worm food. I could trick them into thinking there was a feast waiting for them. Sam said it was easy to trick the eye. The problem was, I didn't know if worms even had eyes. And it would have to be a pretty cheap feast because I needed to save my money for paint. Good thing I didn't have to dish out any money for the statue I had in mind for the front yard. I knew where a few good rocks were hiding at the creek.

Besides reading minds, Miss Steane was a really great teacher. She was nice to everyone: the smart kids and the not-so-smart kids and the not-so-smart kids who thought they were smart.

Like right now, we were supposed to be having a math lesson, but she decided to use the time to talk about fundraising for new playground equipment. She could have talked about it during gym class or art class, but she didn't. She decided to take up time in our math class instead. She knows I hate math. Like I said before, she's the greatest. I didn't really want to talk about raising funds, but it sure beat talking about raising rates and moving decimal points. I bet the teachers at the Whinycat school weren't anywhere near as nice. There was just no way I could go there. There was just no way that I could move. I would rather eat all the worms in my backyard than move from my house.

"The kids in the younger grades really need some new playground equipment," Miss Steane explained. "They need our help. Does anyone have any ideas?"

I had lots of ideas, but I wanted to keep them to myself. My worm-selling idea was a good one, but somehow I doubted the principal would want to fill the whole schoolyard with holes. They could probably make lots of money though, enough for a gigantic new piece of playground equipment. Too bad there wouldn't be any room left for it in the yard because of all the worm holes.

Everyone suggested ideas. Some were pretty dumb, like Tiffany's idea for pet-sitting. Who would want to pay Tiffany to sit with their pet while they were away? She'd probably sit *on* the pet instead of *with* it because she's so clumsy. Come to think of it, I can't understand why they call it "pet-sitting" in the first place. You don't just sit there with a pet. You play with it and take it for a walk to the creek. Same thing with babysitting, although I guess you wouldn't take a baby to the creek.

Unless he liked fishing, of course. Those *sitting* words just didn't make sense. Sometimes words just have a weird language of their own.

I thought my idea was great. We'd sell lottery tickets for people to guess how many times I could bounce a tennis ball off the ceiling and into a garbage can in one week. Of course it would involve me missing some school because the only ceiling that I could use that had the right slant was the one in my bedroom.

"Good idea, but maybe you could practice that trick during the summer," Miss Steane said with a smile. Miss Steane has a nice way of making "No way" sound like "Maybe," even if she doesn't really mean it.

"What about a magic fair?" Sam suggested. He glanced over at me. "We could do card tricks and fortune-telling and optical illusions."

That Sam. What a guy. What a way to sneak in the illusion bit. Now I wouldn't have to think as hard. I was almost jealous of his sneaking-in skill. He usually wasn't that good. He must have been hanging around me too much.

"Why, that's a wonderful idea, Sam," Miss Steane said. "And it fits in perfectly with the unit we're starting in science today. It's on optics." Miss Steane explained what optics was. "Optics is the study of the properties of light, especially the way it changes directions when it's reflected by a mirror or refracted by a lens," she said.

I thought now would be a good time to look smart. There aren't too many of those opportunities floating around. I volunteered my information on refraction. "Sometimes light gets bent out of shape," I said.

Miss Steane was impressed. "Very good, Addison. It's something like that. Do you ever notice on a hot day how the pavement or car roof seems to shimmer? The light looks like it's dancing. That's because it's traveling through hot rising air that has a different density from the air around it. The light is being refracted, or bent, and it looks like it's shimmering. It's the same as a mirage in a desert. The shimmering light from the hot air makes it look like there's a lake on the horizon."

She went on to explain how our eyes can get tricked by all sorts of things. She said that optical illusions are eye tricks caused by weird use of lines or color that make the brain confused. The brain sort of guesses, or fills in the blanks, and comes up with what it thinks is real. I guess my whole life is pretty much an optical illusion, because my brain always has to fill in the blanks. The problem is, it usually comes up with the wrong answer.

"In art class we'll also be learning about illusions," she continued. "Vertical lines guide our eyes upward and horizontal ones guide us outward. There are also ways we can draw pictures to make objects appear farther away. If we draw two lines and make them converge, or come to a point, then it looks like they are receding into the distance, like a set of railway tracks. It's another type of illusion."

Those were good ideas. I didn't need to write them on paper though, because I've got a great memory for things that I can actually use. The problem is, the things that I think are important usually aren't the things my teacher thinks are important. Like right now, when she explained about converging lines and points and guiding our eyes upward, all I could think about was straight-up-and-down lines and sharp points and how I now had a fantastic idea for the front yard. I couldn't wait to get started.

The magic fair was going to be in two weeks, one day before the open house at the new development.

We were going to have a card-trick table, a fortune-telling table, a magic-tricks area, an art-illusion area and a science-optics area. There would be a small admission charge, and we'd sell magic-wand cookies and disappearing juice. Becky was going to do an act with her ventriloquist dummy if she got it clean in time. Some goof had spilled punch all over it a while back. She wanted to clean it up before she gave it back to her uncle, who had let her borrow it. I personally didn't know why it mattered if it was clean or not. It was still worn out and old and creepy. Sort of like some of my great-aunt's old friends.

I was going to be in charge of the invisible-ink trick. That would be easy. I needed to keep my brain free so that I could think of more ways to convince Mom to stay in our old house. Besides, it would be fun to write messages about Tiffany; she wouldn't even know what I was saying.

My head was spinning with ideas on the way home. I was planning to stop at the hardware store to see about buying some cheap paint for the front door, but I decided to stop at the candy store instead. It was time to start solving the break-ins so Mom would feel safer about staying on our street. Solving break-ins meant eating candy. Lots of it. It helped me think. Sam was staying overnight at my house on Friday night so that we could watch out for anything suspicious. I decided that the paint would have to wait. We needed to buy other supplies instead, important stuff like root beer and chips to keep up our strength. I had a feeling we were going to need it. Sometimes you've just got to get your priorities straight.

Chapter Five

Sam came over right after supper the next night. He brought his sleeping bag, his video system and a dozen eggs. I was happy because I thought the eggs were to throw at people, but he told me they were for his science tricks instead. He needed to practice squeezing a peeled hard-boiled egg into a milk bottle. It looked impossible to me. He put some hot water into the bottle, shook it up and then dumped it out. He put the egg on top, and after a little while it dropped inside the bottle. Sam was pretty excited with his magic trick. He went on and on about hot water and air pressure and how it forces air out of the bottle so that the egg could squeeze in. Personally I couldn't see the big deal about sitting there and watching an egg drop into a bottle, but I guess everyone's different. I could think of a whole lot of other things that I'd rather watch than an egg, like maybe the latest dragon-warrior movie or the baseball playoffs on TV or a frog-jumping contest.

To get the egg out, Sam mixed up some vinegar and baking soda and put it in the bottle. He turned it upside down and the egg slipped out. He said the pressure inside the bottle forced the egg back out. Sam kept practicing squeezing that egg into the bottle. I was glad I was doing the invisible-ink stuff. All I had to practice was how to squeeze lemon juice into a bowl without squirting it into my eye.

After I wrote some messages on paper with the lemon juice, Mom helped me iron the paper to make the words appear like magic. Sam told me that the heat makes the lemon juice appear. The acid in the lemon juice weakens the paper. When you heat the paper up, the weakened parts of the paper where the writing was turns brown.

SHOE BOX. The words appeared out of thin air. "Shoe box?" Mom asked as she put away the iron. "What's that got to do with anything?"

"I didn't want to tell you, Mom," I said. "That's the nickname for the new development that you like. People are calling it 'the Shoe Box' because it's so small." It was partly true. Sam and I were calling it that. As far as I knew, we qualified as people.

Mom smiled. "We'll see about that at the open house," she said as she put on her coat. "I've got to go to the astronomy club meeting now, but I should be back about eleven. Make sure you lock the door after me, and don't let anyone in."

"Sure," I said. We weren't going to let anyone in. Well, besides ourselves, that is. We'd need to let ourselves back in after we spied on Becky's house.

"By the way," Mom said as she headed out the door, "what happened to the mirror that was here in the entryway?"

"Oh, I'm borrowing it for the magic show," I confessed. That was partly true. Alex, the skinny kid who sat next to me in class, was going to use it to create some sort of illusion. He was going to lean the mirror up against a table. Then he was going to stand with one leg behind the mirror and the other leg in front of the mirror. He said if he lifted up his front leg it would look like he was floating in the air because you would just see his lifted leg and the image of his lifted leg.

The main reason I took the mirror though was because Sam had said that mirrors make rooms look bigger. They sort of tricked the eye into thinking that there was more space than there really was. I couldn't have Mom thinking our entryway was any bigger than it actually was. I needed all the help I could get. Besides, that mirror was always in the way when I tried to bounce a tennis ball off the wall and out the front door. It would be easier to do now.

After Mom left, Sam showed me some cool optical illusions on the Internet. There were tons of sites. There were some pictures that changed shape right before your eyes if you stared at them long enough. There were others where you'd swear that one line was shorter than the other, but really they were both exactly the same length. It had something to do with arrows at the end of the lines. Some pages had things that looked like they were spinning around when they weren't. One picture of an old man was really creepy. Even though I knew better, I could swear the guy's eyes were following me. There were pictures of staircases that looked crooked but really weren't. I wondered if I could somehow paint the whole house in a way that would make our crooked steps look straight. I found one site that said vertical lines make things look taller. Maybe I could paint stripes on the broken shutters to make them look tall enough to match the windows. Maybe that's why zebras have stripes. They probably like looking taller than they really are so that lions don't chase them as much.

As soon as it got dark, we went outside. I locked the door behind me and we started out. The street was really quiet. A dog barked a few doors down. I jumped a mile. Did you ever notice that when it's dark, noises seem to be a million times louder? I'd swear I could even hear Sam's glasses sliding down his nose as we walked. That's not an optical illusion, it's some other kind. I don't know its name.

We went really slowly so we could watch for anything strange. I was glad there were some cars on the street. That way we didn't feel quite so alone. I let Sam go in front of me. I mean, he wears glasses, so if something jumped out in front of us, he'd be able to see it better than I would. You have to be logical about things like that.

The moon was right above our heads. In a way that was good, because the sidewalks were all lit up. In a way it was bad, because where there's light there are also shadows. Lots of them. I didn't remember the trees being that big before or the bushes that wide or the shadows that gigantic. Who knew what could be hiding in those gigantic shadows?

When we got to Becky's house, we stopped. I closed my eyes and listened. I can hear better when I can't see. Also it made it easier to ignore the creepy garage when my eyes were shut. Sam could do the looking for us both. It wasn't that I was afraid or anything, it's just like I said before—Sam can probably see better because of his glasses.

Everything sounded normal. Well, as normal as everything can sound in the middle of the night on a dead-end street. I opened my eyes just once to look at the house. I could see the light on in the living room. I could see Becky's family watching TV. I could see Sam inspecting the garage. By inspecting, I mean taking three steps up the driveway and then jumping back to the sidewalk.

I decided that was enough. We'd done our bit for crime solving. The crimes would have to solve themselves. We were just about to head home when I noticed something white fluttering in the shrub next to the garage. It looked like a piece of garbage, but I decided to send Sam over to get it anyway. I was sure he wouldn't mind. It might have been a clue to the break-ins.

"Here," he said, shoving the crumpled up paper into my hands. "Next time let's do this when it's light," he whispered. "When it's daytime. When we can see."

I flattened out the paper as much as I could. I shone my flashlight on it. It was just a shred. We could only make out two words.

Sam 11

Those two words jumped off the paper and into our throats. We gasped because we couldn't scream. And then we ran.

Chapter Six

If I'd known that I could run that fast, I would have tried out for the track team. I would have been the hands-down winner. I left Sam in the dust.

I made it back to my house in record time. I waited on the porch for Sam because I'm a nice guy. That and the fact that I'd given him my keys to hold while I read the note.

I took the keys from him and fumbled with them to open the door. We'd really have to get a better light on the porch, because it was hard to see the lock. It didn't help that my hands were shaking, probably from the cold night air.

Once inside, we turned on every light in the house. I could feel the creepiness of the street seeping in through every cracked window and crooked door.

We sat down at the table and looked at the note again. It wasn't Becky's neat writing. These were scrawled letters, even messier than mine. We looked at that note so hard that we didn't even feel like having any root beer or chips.

The note was about Sam. The intruder must have been watching him. He even knew that Sam had just turned eleven. What else did he know about him? He must have gotten Sam's street mixed up with Becky's. Now Sam's street was going to be the unsafe one. Hopefully Sam's mom wouldn't want to move now too.

When Mom got home, we showed her the note. We weren't going to at first, because I didn't want her to be any more scared than she already was. I knew I should show her for Sam's sake though. My mom would tell his mom about it and then he'd feel better. Sam's mom would take care of it. She's very logical, almost as logical as me. Sometimes you've just gotta do what you've gotta do.

Mom didn't seem too concerned. She said that the note could have been anything. Maybe one of Sam's friends wrote it a while ago as a reminder about Sam's birthday. Maybe the man from the corner store was keeping track of all of the kids' ages in the neighborhood. He always gave out free packs of gum on our birthdays. It could have blown there from anywhere, especially in the storm we'd had the week before. She smiled and said not to worry about it. I couldn't tell if it was her "It's really nothing to worry about" smile or her "It's nothing to worry about too much, but I'm a bit worried anyway" smile. I hoped it was the first one. Finding a note about Sam in the schoolyard is one thing. Finding a note about Sam at the site of the break-ins is another story.

Sam decided to go home. Mom made us some chamomile tea, but he didn't feel like drinking it. I downed mine in one fell swoop. It always made me feel sleepy, and that's all I wanted to do. Sleep. Nice and safe in my own room. I'd think about the note tomorrow.

When we got back from driving Sam home, I went to bed. It was nearly midnight. That chamomile tea didn't seem to be working. I had too many ideas swirling through my head. The note was bad enough, but I was running out of time to think of ways to change our house.

For once I wished my room wasn't quite so big. Maybe Mom was right about not needing all this space. If my room were smaller, then I wouldn't have to wonder what might be hiding in the empty space behind the chair where I threw all of my clothes.

I decided to take the clothes off the chair and throw them on the floor instead. That way I could see through the back rails. Better safe than sorry. Then I decided to take the batteries out of the remote-control car in the corner, just in case. I mean, what if the car just started up by itself in the middle of the night? It would wake up Mom for sure. Either the car would wake her up or I would wake her up with my scream when I saw the car moving on its own. Besides, I could use those batteries for the flashlight that I was planning on taking to bed with me.

I was almost asleep when I noticed the mirror that I was going to lend to Alex propped up in the corner. I got up again and flipped it around so it faced the wall. Sometimes mirrors look a whole lot better when there's nothing looking back at you.

I tried one more time to get to sleep, but now my eyelids didn't want to behave. Did you ever notice how your eyelids flutter back and forth really fast when you're trying to be still so you can sleep? The more you want them to stop moving, the faster they jump around. Same with your brain. The more you want it to slow down, the faster ideas and pictures come storming through. Like right now, ripped notes and slimy worms and broken steps were playing hide-and-seek in my head.

I tried counting sheep, but every time the sheep got to the fence, they tripped and fell on the ground instead.

I knew I needed to get at least a few hours of sleep because of the baseball game the next day. I'd need to concentrate to win. Then again, we were playing the Whinycats. The boring, annoying Whinycats and the equally boring, annoying Trent. The only good thing about thinking about Trent was that it finally put me right to sleep.

Chapter Seven

I dragged myself out of bed after the third time Mom called me the next morning. I wished I had felt that tired the night before. I would have slept better. I was too tired to pick the almonds out of the organic muesli to save them for the squirrels. I ate them instead. The squirrels would have to wait. I didn't even have the energy to complain about the pomegranate juice Mom gave me. She knows I only like juices I can spell.

At the game Sam looked tired too. Even his hair looked tired, like he'd been scratching his head and thinking all night.

"Everybody knew I was turning eleven," he said when we got to the field. "My birthday was in February, so I was the first one in the class to turn eleven.

That was a big deal. Mom said somebody just wrote the note to remind them to buy an 'eleven' birthday card, because they were used to everyone turning ten. She said it had nothing to do with Becky's house."

I didn't really buy that explanation. You wouldn't need to write a note to remind yourself that your friend was turning eleven. Maybe Sam's mom wasn't so logical after all. It had to have something to do with the break-ins. Both notes were found there. Becky had turned eleven last month. The intruders couldn't find whatever they were looking for at Becky's, so they were probably going to go to Sam's next. I was glad my birthday wasn't until June. I sure wouldn't want to find my name and age scrawled on a dirty note near a creepy garage that had been broken into. Still, it was nice of Sam's mom to come up with some sort of explanation

"Yeah, that sounds right," I said. Sam was trying to sound sure of himself, but I could tell that he really wasn't. He flares his nostrils three times when he's pretending. I used to think he was just trying to stop his glasses from sliding down his nose, but I know better now. I call it pretending because I doubt that Sam would ever lie. He can pretend with the best of us once in a while though.

The Whinycats looked meaner and whinier than usual. Trent was the catcher, which was good because I didn't have to look at him when I was up to bat. We got through most of the game without giving up a run, but in the eighth inning they complained that our bat was too broken. Too broken? Why they would care if our bat had a couple of pieces missing from the end was beyond me. You'd think they would have realized that it's harder to hit a ball with a broken bat. I guess it gave their mouths something to do. I liked the broken bats. They were lucky. They'd been around forever. Sometimes old things are best. Just like my house.

Their whining must have thrown our team, because the Whinycats tied it up with two runs.

In the bottom of the ninth, I was up to bat with two out. Sam was on third. The pitcher glared at me. Out of the corner of my eye, I saw Trent do one of his fancy little hand signals to the pitcher.

I was just about to swing when I saw Trent jump way over to my right side. I don't know what he was doing there, because that sure wasn't where the ball was. The ball came right at me. It was so low it almost touched the ground. Too low for me to swing at, which was good because it was so fast I would have missed it.

It zoomed right past me and right through the hole in the fence behind me. Good old Trent tried to run around the fence after it, but he shouldn't have wasted his energy. It was too late. I walked to first, and Sam came home from third. We won the game.

Let me tell you, that pitcher was mad. Not at us—we won the game fair and square. He was mad at Trent.

"Good thing that guy's not on our team," I said to Sam on the way home. I almost felt sorry for Trent. Almost.

"Trent got his signals mixed up," Sam explained. "That's why the pitcher was mad. I heard Trent saying that two taps on the glove was a throw-out on his old team. Trent probably thought they would let you walk so that Chris, the next batter, would be up. Everyone knows that poor Chris hasn't had one hit all year. He didn't realize that two taps on the glove on this team means a fastball. It's that illusion thing again. The same thing can have different meanings. It all depends on how you look at it."

I nodded because I was too tired to think. Besides, I didn't have much time to think; I had a busy weekend ahead of me. I was going to spend the rest of the day fixing up the house. I had a great idea for the front yard. It involved some begging for free materials from a few places around town, but I knew it would be worth it. I put on my best begging face and headed downtown.

First up was the hardware store. I managed to get half a can of free paint that some guy had returned because he said it was the ugliest color in the world. I remember Sam saying that everybody sees things differently. I bet that paint would look good on our front door. It would make our house look new and fantastic. Well, new anyway.

After that I went to the sporting-goods store. I managed to get eight broken hockey sticks because the season was over. That, coupled with the two broken bats I already had, would be just perfect.

My last stop was the corner store. I used real money there. I bought five packs of gum. It was for fixing the gate, after I was done chewing it. No sense wasting perfectly good sticky stuff just because it had lost its flavor. You've always gotta be thinking about the environment, you know, recycling and all.

I started with the porch steps. I covered one of the holes with a broken shutter from the shed. I couldn't cover both of the holes, because the squirrels liked to jump through them to get under the porch. I guess I could have built a separate squirrel-jumping hole on the side of the stairs, but that would have been too much work.

I took a break with a can of root beer, and then I spent the next three hours repainting, repairing and replacing. I would have rather been replaying my old video game, but sometimes you've just gotta make the sacrifice. I had to make our property look like a million dollars. It would have been easier to do if I really had a million dollars. I would have filled the yard with neat things like a roller coaster and an arcade. Maybe a miniature golf course would look good next to a fish pond. It's good to think green.

Finally I was finished. I inspected my work. Good thing Mom was at work. I wanted her to be surprised when she saw what I'd done. I had a feeling she was going to be more than surprised. Just how much more was what I was worried about.

Chapter Eight

"What got at your bushes? Some sort of wild animal?" Sam asked when he dropped by the next morning.

I was waiting for Sam out on the sidewalk in front of my house. "Close," I admitted. An animal hadn't attacked the bushes, but I'd spent half an hour cutting those bushes to make them look like animals. I wanted them to look like the ones in the theme parks in Florida. I'd seen commercials with smiling mice and flying elephants greeting happy visitors. I guess they made people feel welcome. Personally, I would rather have free tickets to the park to welcome me instead of a bunch of chopped-up bushes. I thought Mom would like them though. I figured they would take the attention away from the house. I guess the scissors I'd used weren't too sharp because those bushes sure didn't look like animals now. At least not any animal I'd ever seen. Maybe something from a zoo on Mars.

"What happened to your front door?" Sam cried as he stepped past me.

It was nice of Sam to notice the door. I guess he couldn't really not notice it since it was bright orange. I wasn't sure about this illusion stuff and different people seeing different things though. Me and the guy who had bought the paint before both saw the same thing: No matter how you looked at it, that paint was still the ugliest color in the world.

At least the door looked new. The orange didn't match the green shutters of the house, but it did match the new fence.

I guess Sam hadn't noticed the fence yet, because he wasn't saying anything about it. I caught up to him. He was just standing there on the sidewalk, staring at the corner of our yard where the old shed was. I guess he couldn't believe the fact that I had remembered some stuff from science and art class. I remembered how Miss Steane had told us how to make a painting look like a window. I'd painted a picture of a dog on the shed. Then I'd painted a big frame around it, with lines that looked like window panes. It looked like the dog was inside the shed, looking out the window. I knew Mom would feel safer now since we didn't have a real watchdog. Any dog is better than none, even if it is an orange illusion.

Sam's mouth was hanging open. For once he didn't have anything to say. I didn't know if that was a good thing or a bad thing. He turned and looked at the fence.

He just shook his head three times. That Sam. What a guy. Sometimes he just can't come up with the words to describe my great inventions. He's just too impressed.

I had to admit that the fence sure did stand out. I'd wanted something to catch your eye out in front so that you wouldn't look at the old shed so much. Boy, did that fence catch your eye. In fact it caught both eyes without even trying.

That white picket fence in the new development couldn't begin to compare to this one. And it hadn't cost me a penny. All of those broken hockey sticks and bats looked good all lined up with their points stuck in the ground. They were held together with fishing line.

I'd had just enough paint left over from the door and the dog to paint them orange.

"Let's go," Sam finally said, shaking his head once more. I guess he didn't have time to look at the work I'd done on the gate. Good thing, because the gum hadn't really worked all that well. The gate still didn't shut.

Sam was a bit like Mom. When she'd seen the yard last night, she hadn't said anything either. She'd just stared at me and felt my head to see if I had a fever. I got the feeling that she wasn't too pleased. In fact I think it made her want to move out of that house even faster. I didn't get it. The house looked great. What else was I supposed to do? I swear, sometimes the harder I try the worse things get. I guess that explains why usually I try not to try.

Last night I'd overheard her on the phone to the real-estate agent. They were talking about mortgage rates and interest and other weird number stuff. For once I was glad that I was so bad at math. That way I couldn't understand what they were talking about. I didn't really want to know.

Mom hadn't even been impressed when I'd shown her the newspaper article about all the new stoplights and streetlights going up near the new development. I figured new stoplights meant more traffic which meant more idling cars which meant more pollution. I don't think she followed my thinking. It could have been that her brain was confused because she had just tripped over my bike on the way to the bathroom. I had been trying to show her how crowded the townhouse was going to be when I had to store all my outdoor stuff inside. I was starting to think that no matter how awful a picture I painted of the new townhouses, she wasn't going to be swayed. I knew what she was thinking. At least there were no break-ins on the neighboring streets over there, so the area was safe. I was starting to panic.

I grabbed the old wagon from the shed and followed Sam down the street. He was still shaking his head. He was probably kicking himself for not coming up with those decorating ideas himself. I let him pull the wagon to make him feel more important. Heck, I'd probably even let him pull it back after fishing too. It would be filled with rocks from the creek then. I needed materials to build my fantastic statue for the front yard.

I couldn't wait to get to the creek. It would be nice and relaxing to be fishing instead of renovating.

Fishing was fishing. That's why I liked it. It was nothing else. I didn't have to think when I was fishing. I'd tried that before and it didn't work. I think it's because the fish need to be nice and relaxed too if they're going to bite. They can't be relaxed if there's too much stuff going on around them, like thinking and worrying. That meant my brain had to be relaxed. I'm pretty good at a lot of things, but relaxing my brain is one of my specialties.

When we got to the creek, I sold the seven worms that I had dug out of the backyard that morning to some old guy who forgot his bait. I think he forgot his glasses too, because he was doing an awful lot of squinting. Business was looking up. That guy probably didn't even see how many worms he was buying. I probably could have sold him seven pieces of my chewed-up gum instead and he wouldn't have noticed the difference. I would have felt bad for him though. Not to mention the fish. I don't think fish even like gum.

I had just leaned back against the old oak tree and closed my eyes when I heard an annoying voice drifting toward me. I guess *drifting* isn't the right word. A nice soft voice might drift. Tiffany's cackle cut through the air like a dentist's drill. I could hear her little group of friends laughing with her.

"Well, look who's here, the two losers themselves," she said loudly when she got to my tree. "Do you honestly think you're going to catch anything?"

"We might have a chance if you get lost," I said without looking up. It was bad enough that I had to listen to Tiffany. I didn't want to insult two senses at once by having to see her too. "Your voice is enough to scare a whale away."

"Yeah," Sam said quietly.

Tiffany tapped her foot on a tree root. "Those fish are smart. They're going to stay as far away from you as possible."

"Yeah, well maybe you should listen to the fish," I said.

"Maybe if you painted the worms orange you'd have better luck," Tiffany said. Her friends giggled.

She must have seen the house. Tiffany had visited our street two weeks in a row. Wow. How lucky could we get? No wonder the real estate prices were going up.

"We were just at Becky's," she explained, not that I cared. "I wanted to invite her to my birthday party."

Yeah, right. That made about as much sense as me wanting to do some extra homework to raise my marks. Tiffany didn't like Becky. Tiffany's birthday wasn't until the summer. She just needed an excuse to spy on her and try to get some more gossip about the break-ins. Becky would see right through that. People like Tiffany couldn't be tricky if they tried, because they just weren't smart enough to cover the tracks of their tricks.

"Becky's mom found another note," Tiffany gloated, nodding like a bobble-head doll. "There was just a torn piece of paper," she said. "Becky showed it to me. Her dog had been trying to bury it."

Tiffany knew that I was itching to hear what was on the note, but she took her own sweet time telling me. I guess it made her feel important.

"Yeah, well that's nice, but why don't you go for a walk and leave us alone," I suggested, yawning.

"I bet it's got something to do with money or metal," she continued. "The note was just two words. *Coin* and *pin*. The last note said *8 cents*."

Tiffany had a one-track mind, which was probably good because her brain probably couldn't handle two tracks at once. Also, she had no clue about the note that said *Sam 11,* and I wasn't about to tell her. "Yeah, well maybe it was a list of ideas for a fair, like a coin toss and a knock-over-the-bowling-pin game that cost eight cents to play." I was proud of myself for coming up with that one so fast. "Of course you wouldn't know about games like that, because you're about as athletic as this worm," I added as I tossed it at her.

"You're just stupid, Addison," Tiffany muttered as she stomped away.

Stupid or not, at least I knew how to get rid of annoying people. Now all I had to do was get rid of the annoying problems that were floating around my head. There were only seven days until the open house. Was Mom seeing our place in a new light yet? Sure, I hadn't made much from the worm-digging business yet, but things were bound to pick up in the summer. Did she see that we really did need all that room? Did she see how easily you could fix things up to make the place look better? Did she feel safer on the street? Plus there was something else bugging me. There was something about those dumb notes that seemed familiar. I didn't know exactly what it was yet, but there was an idea simmering in my brain that hadn't come to the front yet. My brain takes its time to simmer.

I decided to put everything aside and think about it tomorrow. My dad had once said that things always look better in the morning. I sure hoped my ideas did. And my house too.

Chapter Nine

On Friday morning we had a rehearsal for the magic fair the next day. I was glad it was almost the weekend. I had been busy all week, building my statue in the front yard and improving my worm-selling operation in the backyard. I even impressed myself.

The practice meant that math class was cancelled again. It was my lucky day. Science class too, although I couldn't complain too much about that one. I sort of liked the stuff we had been doing recently in science. We were still learning about optics. One day Miss Steane gave us each a shiny spoon. I thought we were going to get some ice cream to go with it, but she had something different in mind. She told us about lenses. A convex lens, like a doorknob, curves outward.

A concave lens, like a bowl, turns inward. We looked at our reflection in the spoons. My face was upside down when I looked at the bowl of the spoon. When I got really close to it my face was suddenly right-side up! When I looked at the other side of the spoon my face was really long or really fat, depending on how I turned the spoon. It was like the spoon was tricking me. Optics was pretty cool. Anytime you could trick somebody into thinking something else was pretty neat.

Everyone practiced their magic tricks for the class. Lynne showed us how to do this cool trick with a paper-towel roll. You hold the tube up to one eye and then put the palm of your other hand about one inch away from the end of the tube. With both eyes open, you focus on something across the room. Then it looks like there's a hole in the middle of your hand.

Claire was the fortune-teller. She had a big round marble that she was using as a crystal ball. I was going to see if I could borrow it after the fair. It would look great on top of my statue. Claire said she could read palms and tell your future by looking at the lines on them. I wondered what she would be able to see from the two twisted scars on my palm from when I got a fishhook stuck in it. Probably she'd be able to predict that I wouldn't try pulling a fishhook out of a tree anytime soon.

John and David, the brainy twins in our class, had set up a whole optics table. They used stuff from a science kit one of them got for Christmas. I don't know why anyone would ask for a science kit as a present. Maybe they thought it was some kind of a video game. The experiments were sort of fun though. They made a blue sky appear by shining a flashlight on a mixture of milk and water in a pop bottle. They said it was because the mixture scattered more blue wavelengths than any other color. Then they made a pinhole camera out of an old potato-chip canister. I had lots of empty pop bottles and chip tins hiding under my bed. I could probably make tons of money by selling my own science kits. I stored that idea away for later.

Scott did a trick with disappearing Easter eggs. He showed me how he did it. He used something called the French drop. He pretended to drop the egg into his left hand and then steal it with his right hand. When he opened up his right hand the egg wasn't there because it was still in his left hand, which by now was in his pocket. Then he pulled the egg out of his pocket and showed everyone. I could have made those chocolate eggs disappear faster than he did in just one gulp.

Sam did his own egg trick for the class. He was pretty nervous for some reason. How could you be nervous about stuffing an egg into a bottle? I've had lots of experience with stuffing eggs. I don't like them, organic or not. When Mom serves a hard-boiled one for lunch at home, I stuff it into my jeans pocket. When I get outside, I toss it to the dog next door. He doesn't like it either, but at least he can bury it. I tried it once with a fried egg but my jeans didn't look so good afterward.

There was going to be an intermission with cookies and punch at the fair. Chris would play the guitar, and Tiffany and her friends had made up a dance, something about genies. I'd have to make sure I did a vanishing act before that. After the intermission Miss Steane was going to present a slide show about optical illusions, and then Becky and her nice, clean ventriloquist's dummy were doing their act.

I was lucky because my invisible-ink trick was easy. It didn't take much time to do, so I got to watch everyone else practice.

The fair was going to be held in the library, but we were storing the props and supplies in our classroom. We spent the afternoon decorating the library with mirrors and cards and magician hats. It was a big improvement over books.

On the way home from school, Sam and I walked over to the other side of town to get a closer look at the new development. There was only one finished townhouse, which was being used as a display model. From what I could see, it was ugly, statue and all. And it was small. There wasn't one tree in the whole field where the townhouses were going to go, unless you counted a scrawny little bush beside the statue. What would a home without trees be like? Probably as bad as a creek without fish.

To top it all off, we ran into Trent near the new development. He was so surprised to see us that he dropped his backpack on his foot. He yelped and picked it up. Then he just glared at us and walked away as fast as he could.

"I guess he's still mad because we won the game," I said as I watched him practically run down the street.

"Yeah, he's probably going home to study his signals," Sam said loudly when Trent was far enough away not to hear him. Sam's not as brave as I am.

I noticed that Trent had dropped something on the sidewalk. It was a magazine. "Wait, you forgot your magazine!" I yelled. Trent just kept going. He must have still been really mad. I picked up the magazine and flipped through it. It was a collectors' magazine, full of old stuff like books and toys and puppets. Why anyone would want to collect stuff like that was a mystery to me. I had tons of junk lying around my room. I didn't need to add any more old stuff. I'd rather have new stuff, like new gaming systems. I did collect the odd sports card or two. Cards don't take up much room, and they left more space on the floor for my video games.

That night I played my Ancient Warrior game for two straight hours. I didn't want to think about Becky and burglars and notes and poor Sam. I didn't want to think about real estate. I wanted to think about real *escapes* instead. There's something about fighting two-headed dragons that makes you forget about your other problems. Besides, I needed to practice my eye-hand coordination for the magic fair tomorrow.

I wanted to make my invisible-ink trick look good. Maybe if I got good enough at writing invisible notes, I would be even better at figuring out what the visible ones meant.

Chapter Ten

The next day was nice and sunny. It was a great day for fishing. Too bad we had to spend the whole afternoon setting up for the magic fair. Nobody should have to go to school on the weekend. I guess this one time was okay though, as long as they didn't make a habit out of it.

The fair started at seven o'clock in the evening. A ton of people came to it, mostly the families of all the kids at school. Some of the teachers brought their families. Unfortunately Tiffany brought her whole family, even her cousin Trent. My mom came too. She was in a good mood, probably thinking about the open house the next day.

The fortune-telling booth went over well. People paid a whole bunch just to hear that they would be going on a trip someday or that they might win some money. The optics-experiments table had a lot of people around it. The 3-D glasses were really popular. Alex did his mirror trick, and people liked it. I guess everyone likes to be tricked once in a while.

Sam was up next. Poor Sam. He gets nervous at the drop of a hat. Well, at the drop of an egg, in this case. His hands were so sweaty that the egg that was supposed to drop in the bottle slid through his fingers and dropped on the floor instead, just in front of Mrs. Wilson, Tiffany's mom. She tried to jump aside but landed on the egg instead when it rolled, probably because her feet are so big. Good thing it was hard-boiled instead of soft. Her heel was covered in a crumbly yolk, and that was the end of that trick. And the end of her new shoes, by the sound of her complaints.

I was the last act before intermission, right after Chris and his magic-hat trick. Since my trick took so little time, I was in charge of getting the props out of the classroom for the second part of the show.

Everybody else got to stay in the library and eat cookies. Everyone except for Trent, that is. I'd seen him sneak out. I guess having to watch Tiffany do her genie dance during the intermission was too much even for him.

Chris started doing his trick. I yawned. It was so boring. He was really slow. All he had to do was say a few words and pull a fake rabbit out of a hat that had a secret compartment in it. Now if it had been a real rabbit, it would have been more exciting. Or maybe a real fish. That would have been even better. He messed up the trick and had to start over. I guess the rabbit was stuck in the secret compartment. If he had used a real fish, it would have just jumped right out of that hat.

I started daydreaming after he started the trick over again for the third time. My eyes drifted over to the bulletin boards beside me. Since it was the library, there were book reports and projects about authors plastered all over the wall. There was one bulletin board that featured authors from different countries.

Chris started the trick again, this time shaking the hat to make sure everything was working properly.

I looked back again at that last bulletin board.

There was something there that caught my eye. I closed my eyes so that I could concentrate better. There was definitely something jumping around in my head, wanting to get out. Something big. I closed my eyes even tighter so that whatever it was could make its way to the front of my brain. I thought about the baseball game and the secret signals. I thought about magazines and streets. I thought about the disappearing-egg act. Suddenly the things that were simmering in my brain started to boil over.

Bit by bit, things bubbled up and became clear. So clear they almost popped right out of my head. I kicked myself. Why hadn't I seen them before?

Chris was still saying his magic words. I looked around quickly for Becky. I saw her at the back of the library, biting her nails and tapping her feet. She must have been super-nervous about her ventriloquist act. The last time she did it, it was a disaster.

I crept back to her.

"Becky, quick, over here," I whispered. We didn't have much time. I needed to see if I was right. We hid behind the magazine stacks.

"Where did you say you got your dummy from?" I asked.

"My uncle picked it up at a yard sale. It was really cheap because it's so old."

"Yeah, well, that's one way of looking at it," I said. "Where did you keep it before it got cleaned up?"

"In the garage. Why?"

I nodded. "I thought so. One last question. Tiffany's cousin, Trent. He just moved here last month. Do you know where he came from?"

Becky thought for a minute. "It was from a different province. Quebec, I think."

I knew it. I thanked Becky and then ran for the door.

"Wait! You're up next!" she cried.

"I can't!" I yelled. They'd have to do without me. I had more important things to do. Things like solving the break-ins and keeping my house.

I got out of the library in time to see him running to the exit at the end of the hallway. It looked like he had something hidden under his bright orange jacket.

I was glad that I'd had all of that running practice in baseball. I was fast. I'd catch up to him in no time.

Trent didn't stand a chance.

Chapter Eleven

"Trent!" I yelled as I raced down the hallway. "Wait!"

Trent looked back once and then pushed open the door. He ran across the yard and out to the corner of the street. He paused for a split second, like he was waiting for someone. That split second almost gave me time to catch up to him. Almost, but not quite.

"Get back here!" I yelled.

He took off like the spaceship in my video game. One second he was there, and the next he was gone. I guess all that running in baseball helped him too.

He ran so fast that I couldn't catch up to him. He ran down Pine Street, up Oak Street and across Elm Street. When he got finished with the tree streets, he started on the others. I couldn't see any pattern to where he was going, sort of like I can't see a pattern to stuff I learn in math. I think he was trying to confuse me. It takes a lot more than that.

The light was fading fast. Soon it would be dark. We were in my neighborhood now. He headed toward my street and started to slow down. He must have been getting tired. I bet he was glad that I lived on a corner lot, because he decided to cut right across my lawn to get to the street on the other side of it.

Now I don't like to brag or anything, but sometimes I do stuff that comes in handy later, even if people don't appreciate it at the time. All of my hard work in the yard paid off. Just not how I expected it to.

You can't say I didn't try to warn him. "Trent, wait!" I yelled one more time as I saw his orange back disappearing into the almost-dark yard. That was the last thing I saw of him. I heard him loud and clear though.

"Aaaaaaaaah! Help!" I don't know which was louder, Trent's voice or the sound of the stones from the statue crashing down. I guess I should have used better glue to hold them together. The chewed-up gum hadn't worked too well there either.

You can't say that Trent wasn't stubborn. He limped to the gate and disappeared into the backyard.

I guess he thought he could jump over the fence into the neighbor's yard and lose me.

By now I had almost caught up to him. I could hear Mom's voice behind me. She must have seen me racing out of the school. I pushed past the open gate just in time to hear Trent scream one last time.

I guess he didn't see the big hole in the backyard. Of course he might have been distracted by the mirror that I had hung with fishing line from the old pine tree. I'd wanted the worms to think that the feast that I'd left for them was even bigger than it really was. Most of the holes that I'd dug in the yard were small, but I thought that maybe if I dug just one super-big hole I might get super-big worms coming to it. Worms might like more space. Sort of like how I liked more space to live in. I guess Trent's foot hadn't liked that much space though. It got stuck in there, and he went flying into the worm feast of eggshells and banana peels. So did his parcel.

I quickly stepped over Trent and picked up what he had dropped.

I didn't need light to see what it was. Even though I knew better, I could swear that dummy's eyes were moving.

Chapter Twelve

"You did it!" Sam cried as he slapped me on the back. "You figured it out! You solved the crime!"

Sam had come over right after his breakfast the next morning to congratulate me. His mom had told him the news when he'd woken up.

I poured more syrup on my super-big stack of pancakes. Mom had made an extra big batch today and had even added some organic chocolate bits. I offered some pancakes to Sam.

"How did you know it was Trent? How did you know it was the dummy he wanted? How did you figure everything out?" Sam asked in between gulps of juice.

That Sam. He knew I couldn't answer three things at once. I guess he was too excited to think.

"Well, Sam," I said, "it was actually something you said that started things simmering in my brain."

Sam looked puzzled. I took another bite of pancake and leaned back. It was nice taking my time to explain things. My brain had gone from simmering to boiling. Now it could slow down.

"Well, you see, it was all of that refraction stuff, looking at things from a different angle, from a different point of view," I explained. "There really are a lot of optical illusions floating around."

"I still don't get it," Sam confessed.

Wow. It sure felt different being the smart one. Kind of nice for a change. I wouldn't want to get used to it though. It was too much work figuring things out and explaining them to everybody. Sometimes it was easier to just play dumb and sit back and listen.

"Remember when Trent got his signals mixed up at the baseball game?" I asked.

Sam nodded.

"Well, I didn't think anything of it at the time, except that he needed to get his signals straight. Then remember when we ran into him and he dropped that magazine?"

Sam nodded again. "Yeah—it was a collectors' magazine with old toys and puppets," he said.

"Dummies are puppets," I said. "I saw a picture of a dummy like Becky's in that magazine when I flipped through it. I didn't think anything of it at the time. Except of course that Trent was dumb to be interested in dummies."

"So Trent was interested in dummies, specifically Becky's dummy. But how does that explain anything else?" Sam asked.

I poured myself a handful of chocolate chips. "We know that Becky's family keeps all sorts of junk from yard sales. Including the dummy. Trent knew that too. What he didn't know was that the dummy was hidden in Becky's closet. She hadn't wanted her uncle to see it until she finished cleaning it. The first time he tried to 'borrow' it from the shed, he must have looked through the shed window and seen the old mannequin heads that Becky's mom keeps there, and guessed that the dummy was there too." Becky's mom likes to make weird art out of anything.

Mom had filled me in on the details of Trent's plans that morning after she had talked to Becky's mom. Now I filled Sam in. It seems that Becky had told Trent that her uncle had only paid fifty dollars for the dummy. Trent had told his friends about it. One of them had just done a school project on ventriloquists. He thought the dummy was worth more. A lot more. Trent did some research and found out just how much more. He said that he was just trying to "borrow" the dummy to get it appraised, but you'd have to be pretty gullible to believe that fishy story.

Sam scratched his head and then his nose. Then he scratched his chin.

"So then Trent tried to break into the garage. I still don't understand how you figured things out. What about the notes?"

I smiled. That was the good part. "Think about it, Sam. Remember what you said. Sometimes things are completely different, depending on how you look at them. Even words. *Sam 11* didn't have anything to do with you or your birthday. It did have something to do with a specific day though."

I let the words sink in. They didn't have too far to sink with Sam though. He caught on pretty quickly. Like I said before, he's a smart guy.

Sam's face lit up like a firecracker. "French!" he yelled. "Those words are French! *Sam 11*! The magic fair was on Saturday, May 11. *Samedi* is French for Saturday! *Sam* for short." Sam looked pleased with himself. And relieved.

I nodded before I gulped down the last of my orange juice. "Yep. I realized it during the magic show. That bulletin board in the library came in handy. I got to thinking about the authors from different countries, and how the same word means different things, depending on how you look at it. Sort of like how Trent's old baseball signals meant something completely different to his new team. Then I started thinking about those notes. Eight cents means eight cents to us. But to the French, *cent* means hundred. That dummy was worth eight hundred dollars. Trent must have been writing the notes to his friends in French so that nobody would figure out what he was planning."

I shook my head. That dummy probably had more brains than Trent did. "That note must have fallen out of Trent's pocket the next week when he tried to sneak into Becky's garage," I explained. "He met his friends there, but the dummy was still in Becky's closet, and the garage was locked. They tried to pry to the lock open but it wouldn't work. Then Trent wrote down the date of the magic fair and gave it to his friends. He knew the dummy would be there for sure. He was planning on sneaking it out to them."

I threw my dishes in the sink. "But Becky's dog got that note and ripped it apart. Becky found the first part about eight cents. We found the second part about *Sam 11*. Becky's mom found the third part about *coin* and *pin*, right before the dog tried to bury it."

Sam cut in. "But what do *coin* and *pin* have to do with it?"

Sam almost had it. I tried to be patient, but I knew the creek was waiting. I picked up my fishing pole and headed out the door. Sam followed.

"Think about it, Sam," I urged as we walked to the creek. I pointed to the street sign as we rounded the corner.

Suddenly Sam knew. "*Pin*! That's Pine in French. Our school is on the corner of Pine Street. *Coin* is corner! Those were the directions to the magic fair!"

Sam slapped me on the back. "What a way to figure it out! What a way to solve it! What a way to think!" he gushed as we arrived at the creek.

Yeah, I guess it was a good way to think. Too much thinking for my liking though. Now it was time to fish. Like I said before, fishing and thinking don't go together. I was sure I could fit in a little gloating though. Gloating doesn't take up a whole lot of energy. Just as long as I kept the gloating to myself.

Chapter Thirteen

The next day after school, I found Mom out in the front yard. She hadn't said much about the open house the day before. I figured she didn't want to look too excited about it for my sake. She probably felt sorry for me.

Mom was just finishing throwing the stones from the fallen statue into the old wheelbarrow. I guess she wanted me to take them back to the creek.

"I'll take those back after supper," I said as I helped her push the old wheelbarrow to the shed.

"Back would be good," she said as she wiped her hands on her jeans. "The backyard, that is. I think these stones would make a great rock garden."

Why Mom would want to make a rock garden out of these old stones was a mystery to me. She wouldn't be able to see it from the new townhouse.

"Here," she said as she tossed me a package.

I thought it might be gum by the shape of it. I opened it up. It was a bunch of flower seeds. Why would I want some dumb flower seeds? I scratched my head and then my nose. I was beginning to feel like Sam.

"No use letting all of those perfectly good holes in the backyard go to waste," she said. "Now these seeds have someplace to go."

We headed toward the house. "One more thing," she added as we went inside. "You didn't get to do your invisible-ink trick at the magic fair. Here's your note. I found it upstairs."

It was nice of Mom to think about me. She probably thought I had put a lot of work into it when really it had only taken about thirty seconds. Well, maybe forty if you count the time I had to spend cleaning up the lemon juice after I'd accidentally spilled it in the sugar bowl. I'd been mixing up a bit of lemonade while I was writing the note. No sense wasting perfectly good lemon juice on paper alone.

Mom handed me the note and the iron, which she'd just unplugged.

I felt stupid doing the trick for just one person, but I shrugged and started anyway. I guess Mom was hard up for entertainment.

"Sometimes things seem different, depending on how you look at them," I said. "You probably see a plain piece of paper. I, however, see something else. Concentrate hard and letters will appear right before your very own eyes."

I ran the iron over the paper and waited for the words *Optical Illusion* to appear. I hoped I had spelled them right.

The two words slowly came into view. They weren't the words I was watching for, or even the words I was waiting for, but they sure were the words that I'd been wishing for all along.

I rubbed my eyes to make sure they weren't playing tricks on me and then I read the words out loud.

"*Welcome home*."

I looked up at Mom. "This isn't my note," I said. "What's going on?"

"You're not the only one who can write invisible notes, you know." She laughed and looked out the window at the hockey-stick fence. "You've made quite a mess around here, but you got me thinking."

I guess some people would call it a mess. I called it a masterpiece. "I was just trying to make the house look better. I wanted you to look at it from a different angle," I said.

"That's just it," she pointed out. "I did look at it from a different angle. From a different point of view. Yours."

I held my breath and stopped chewing my gum.

"You went to all of this effort," she continued. "It's obvious how much this place means to you. I never realized it until now, after seeing the place through your eyes. And now that the break-ins have been solved, the street feels safe again."

I started chewing.

"I think we should just stay here," she said as she dumped her organic rice into the pot.

I started breathing.

"Besides," she added, "how could I possibly see the stars at night with all of the lights in the new development? And how could we fit all our outdoor things into that little townhouse? And it would cost more in gas for me to get to work. I'm going to be putting in some extra hours at the downtown office. And just think about all of those horrible stop lights." She rolled her eyes and shook her head.

Right, Mom. Hadn't I told her all of that stuff before? I was so happy that I didn't even point that out. I guess some people take a while to let things sink in, the way it takes a while for water to sink into a wormhole.

I grabbed my hole digger from where I'd been storing it under the kitchen table and headed outside.

"Watch out for that gate," Mom called after me. "It doesn't seem to close too well."

I couldn't wait to plant those seeds. If Mom wanted a flower garden and a rock garden to make the place look better, I could do it easily. I was handy at stuff like that.

I looked up at the trees and ran through the yard. It's strange how sometimes you just feel like flying.

Yep, this place had potential. I would keep a corner of the yard for my worm business. Maybe I could try an ant farm under the pine tree. Plus there were lots more treasures that I needed to bury, like the old brass button that had fallen off the dummy's shirt when Trent fell into the hole in my yard.

I started digging. I would make our place look like a mansion, heck, a castle. A big one. As big as I wanted. I'd get Sam to help me. I'd already proven that two sets of eyes are better than one.

Ideas started dancing in front of me like a shimmering mirage. I could just see it now. Some people would soon call our house a mansion. Some people, like Tiffany, would call it a dump. Like I said before, it all depends on how you look at it. I didn't really care what it was called. As long as it was still called home.

Melody DeFields McMillan is a teacher who lives in Simcoe, Ontario, not far from where she grew up. She is the mother of two adult children. When she's not writing, she's enjoying all that nature has to offer. Her first book about the irrepressible Addison, *Addison Addley and the Things That Aren't There*, was nominated for a Silver Birch Award.